Winnie the Pooh

Pooh's Honey Adventure

By Lisa Ann Marsoli

Illustrated by Disney Storybook Artists

DISNEP PRESS

NEW YORK

Buzz

Buzz Buzz

Based on the "Winnie the Pooh" works by A.A. Milne and E.H. Shepard

First Edition
Library of Congress Cataloging-in-Publication Data on file.
ISBN 978-1-4231-3593-7

8 7 6 5 4 3 2

J689-1817-1-11236

Manufactured in the USA
For more Disney Press fun, visit www.disneybooks.com

 loves honey.

Pooh

He loves the way it looks.

He loves the way it smells.

He loves the way it tastes!

goes to his .

Pooh   cupboard

He wants a sweet snack.

Every in his is empty.

honeypot   cupboard

Hum-dee-dum-doo! No honey

for !

Pooh

goes to his Thoughtful Spot.

Pooh

He thinks about how hungry he is.

He thinks about eating yummy honey.

He thinks about where to get some more!

"I'll look for honey in the
honey  !" says  .

tree

Pooh

8

finds honey.

Pooh

It belongs to some bees.

They do not want to share!

Hum-dee-dum-doo! No honey

for !

Pooh

 keeps looking.

Pooh

His tummy rumbles louder.

thinks he sees a .

Pooh honeypot

It is really his shadow.

Hum-dee-dum-doo! No honey for !

Pooh

Suddenly, everything is made of honey.

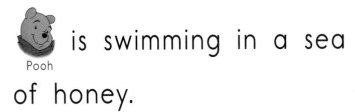Pooh is swimming in a sea of honey.

Then his daydream ends.

Hum-dee-dum-doo! No honey for  !

Pooh

 stops at .

Pooh   Eeyore's house

He looks around for honey.

"My tummy sure is rumbly,"

 says.

Pooh

"Have some of these thistles,"

says  .

Eeyore

Pooh wants something else.

He draws a picture as a hint.

"That honey looks tasty," says

Eeyore
. "I wish I had some."

Hum-dee-dum-doo! No honey

for !

Pooh

continues on his way.

He spots a !
honeypot

There is nothing inside.

Hum-dee-dum-doo! No honey

for !
Pooh

He goes to see .

Christopher Robin

There is no one at home.

Hum-dee-dum-doo! No honey

for  !

Pooh

Then  visits Owl.
Pooh

Hooray!

There is a big  at Owl's
honeypot

house!

"Sorry,  ," says Owl.

Pooh

"I am saving that for later."

Hum-dee-dum-doo! No honey
for  !

Pooh

 meets .
Pooh   Piglet

"Do you know where I can

find some honey?" asks.
                                    Pooh

"Yes," replies . "Here in
                        Piglet

this ."
        tree

 tries to get some honey
Piglet

for  .
Pooh

 gets stuck.
Piglet

Rabbit comes along.

He pulls  out.
Piglet

Then he puts the beehive back

in the .
tree

Hum-dee-dum-doo! No honey

for  !
Pooh

Next, the friends walk past a stream.

A 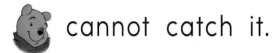 is floating past.
honeypot

 cannot catch it.
Pooh

Hum-dee-dum-doo! No honey for  !
Pooh

"Look!"  cries.
Pooh

A (honeypot) is flying by.

 chases it.
Pooh

He cannot catch it.

"Honey is in such a hurry today!" says  .

Pooh

Hum-dee-dum-doo! No honey for  *!*

Pooh

spots another .

Pooh honeypot

He dips in a paw.

Nothing comes out.

Hum-dee-dum-doo! No honey

for  !

Pooh

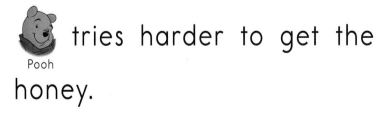 tries harder to get the

Pooh

honey.

It does not come out!

"Hold on," says .
Piglet

He returns with their friends.

Everyone helps remove the honeypot.

Then  gives a present.

Christopher Robin   Pooh

It is a full honeypot!

Hum-dee-dum-doo! NOW

there's honey for  !

Pooh

That night, 's tummy and
Pooh
dreams are full of honey, too!